<u>Christmas With the Gnomes</u> was created from memories of Christmases spent with our wonderful grandparents (Carl Severn and Anna Barr Helgeson) and our parents (Joseph and Inez Smith).

I0526952

<u>Christmas With the Gnomes</u> is dedicated to my siblings, parents, and grandparents. It reflects the beautiful memories that we made at Christmas.

With love to My Homies:

Jim, Joe, Mike, Pat, Barb, Kathy, Linda, and Jeanne

Each one of you helped shape the person I am today.

I love you.

Twinkling lights so shiny and bright,
Hang on the tree to the Gnomes' delight.

A wiggle, a jiggle, we all start to giggle.
A nod to the left, a nod to the right,
soon it will be Christmas night.

Barb and Kathy put bright bows on the presents.

The house smells of sugar cookies, pine trees, and pheasant.

Mom and dad synchronize the music with light while Mike and Pat make a snow fort just right.

A wiggle, a jiggle, we all start to giggle.
A nod to the left, a nod to the right,
soon it will be Christmas night.

St. Nick will be here in a couple of days,

With the hustle and bustle we're all in a daze.

Linda and Jeanne do figure eights
on the ice rink in the back yard,

while Nancy finishes her annual Smith letter that goes in her Christmas card.

A wiggle, a jiggle, we all start to giggle.
A nod to the left, a nod to the right,
soon it will be Christmas night.

We go to Grandpa and Grandma's house.

Grandpa reads a story about a holiday mouse.

Jim and Joe remind us
that Saint Nick is shy.
He will not stop
if he sees us nearby.
So....
down the stairs we go.

Grandpa gives a shout, "All clear."

"Hooray! Hooray!" nine voices cheer.

Surely Saint Nick has just been here.

Up the stairs we quickly run,
Christmas Eve is so much fun.

A wiggle, a jiggle, we all start to giggle.
A nod to the left, a nod to the right,
finally it is Christmas Eve night.

With hoots and hollers
and shouts of joy,
we unwrap "Grammy Jammies"
and a homemade toy.

Giving kisses and hugs
we pack up the car,
stare out the window,
"Look, a tree with a star!"

A wiggle, a jiggle, we all start to giggle.
A nod to the left, a nod to the right,
it is Christmas Eve night.

Back at our home we ask,
"Why does Saint Nick come to us twice?"
Mom smiles and says,
"Because you're so nice."

We jump into our beds
and sweet dreams fill our heads.

A wiggle, a jiggle, we all start to giggle.
A nod to the left, a nod to the right,
now it is Christmas Eve night!

Saint Nick puts presents under the tree.
Of course we wonder what they will be.

Before he goes up the chimney, we'll hear
his famous magical holiday cheer...

"Ho! Ho! Ho!"

A wiggle, a jiggle, we all start to giggle.
A nod to the left, a nod to the right,
now it is Christmas Eve night.

Saint Nick is singing his sweet Christmas song,

So now let's all join along...

"Ho! Ho! Ho!"

A wiggle, a jiggle, we all start to giggle.
A nod to the left, a nod to the right,
now it is Christmas Eve night.

We awake to find presents under the tree

that Saint Nick left there for my siblings and me.

A wiggle, a jiggle, we all start to giggle.
A nod to the left, a nod to the right,
What a Christmas delight.

Merry Christmas and Happy New Year Homies,

With love from all of your Gnomies.

The End!

About the Author
and
the Illustrator

Author: Nancy Villabona

Nancy is a retired teacher and author of Villabona Voyager Books.

She has always loved writing and enjoys sharing that passion with others. This is Nancy's first collaboration with illustrator Sarra Brassard.

Illustrator: Sarra Brassard

Sarra is a college graduate that has a passion for art. She loves the idea of inspiring young minds through art. Sarra hopes to continue growing her creative career.

The real Carl Severn Helgeson and Anna Barr Helgeson

Grandpa and Grandma

My Homies: The Smiths

Back: Pat, Joe, Jim, Mike
Middle: Jeannie, Barb,
Inez Helgeson Smith (Mom),
Joseph Smith (Dad), Kathy, Linda
Front: Nancy

www.ingramcontent.com/pod-product-compliance
Lightning Source LLC
Chambersburg PA
CBHW041542240626
47164CB00002B/106